Ghost Games

by Jana Novotny Hunter
Pictures by Sue Porter

A Doubleday Book for Young Readers

A Doubleday Book for Young Readers

Published by Delacorte Press
Bantam Doubleday Dell Publishing Group, Inc.
666 Fifth Avenue, New York, New York 10103

Doubleday and the portrayal of an anchor with a dolphin
are trademarks of Bantam Doubleday Dell Publishing Group, Inc.

This edition was first published in Great Britain in 1991
by Orchard Books under the title *Luna the Little Ghost*.
Text copyright © 1991 by Jana Novotny Hunter
Illustrations copyright © 1991 by Sue Porter

Library of Congress Cataloging in Publication Data
Hunter, Jana Novotny.
    Ghost games/Jana Novotny Hunter; pictures by Sue Porter.
        p.   cm.
    Summary: After searching for a playmate, a little ghost finds a
real girl and together they play ghost games all through the night.
    ISBN 0-385-30701-2
    [1. Ghosts – Fiction.] I. Porter, Sue, ill. II. Title.
PZ7.H9168Gh   1992
[E] – dc20   91-32416
                                                                   CIP
                                                                    AC

Manufactured in Belgium
February 1993
10 9 8 7 6 5 4 3 2 1
ORC

In the churchyard it is dusky night.
Rosy mists cloud the moon. Bats swoop
in the shadows. Silent and soft, a shape
drifts across the graves... searching.
The shape hovers.
"Whoooooo...?" it moans.

It is a silvery shape. Sometimes it stretches, long and thin, like steam. Sometimes it shrinks to raindrop size. Then it bounces around the churchyard like a raindrop bubble.

What is this silvery shape?
And why does it search?
Is it steam?
Is it a raindrop?
Is it a bubble?

No! It's...

...a ghost!

Luna, the little ghost.

Mischievous Luna,
full of spooky fun,
silvery Luna,
playful as a bubble.
Are you searching
for a playmate tonight?

Little Luna does not speak. She dances around the churchyard. She hides behind a headstone, then out she peeps.

"*Yes!*"

She drifts across the churchyard, to the shadowy farm.

She fades…then takes shape again. And floats to a moonlit barn.

"Whoᵒᵒᵒooo . . . ?" Luna moans as a giant shadow looms.

"Whooo-hooo…?" Luna hoots as the cow waves her tail.

"**Moo, moo**!" bellows the cow.

Luna backs away. "Boo-hoooooo," she seems to say as she floats off toward the little house, the little wooden house where…

... the dog dozes.

Luna hovers, spins, then suddenly swoops.

"Aaoooo!" the dog howls, backing inside his kennel.

"Grrraaooooo!" he growls.
"Boo-hooo…" Luna seems
to howl as she drifts away.

She floats toward the big house, the
house near the moonlit barn. The house
the dog guards.

"Whoooooo...!" Luna moans.

She peers through the window to the
hallway, where shadows stretch like
fingers.

No one stirs.

"Whooooooo . . . ?" Luna wails.
Light as a bubble, she fades through
the wall.

Silent and soft, she floats up, up the stairs…

…into a room…a cozy room…

…where a child sleeps.

Luna drifts close to the sleeping child. She hovers.

The child shivers, stirs, awakes, and rubs sleepy eyes.

"Little ghost? Little ghost, is that you?"
Luna shimmers. "Y-e-e-e-s."

"Little ghost, what do you want?"
asks the child.

"Ooo-ooo." Luna flaps and spins.

"Oooo-ooo-oo." She circles the ceiling
and dances about.

"Little ghost, do you want…some
spooky fun?"

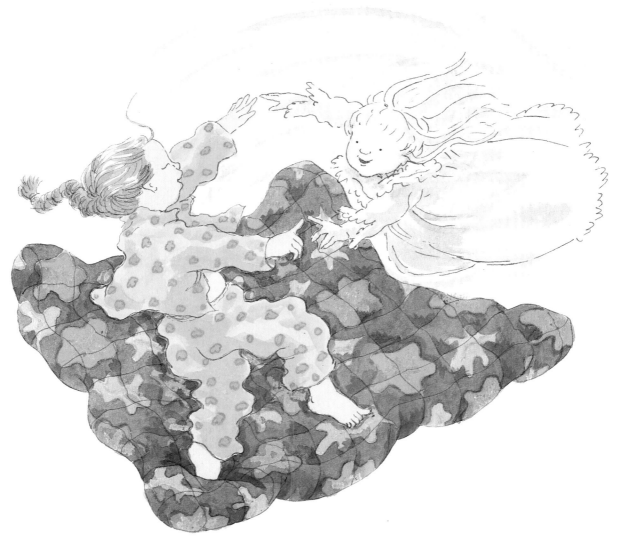

Luna, excited, shimmers and seems
to say, "Y-e-e-e-s."

The child smiles. "Spooky, scary,
midnight fun?"

"*Whoo-hoo!*" Luna hoots, flapping
for joy. She circles the ceiling and spins
around, making shadows loom.

The child hides under the sheets…
makes shadows loom…and dances for
joy on the bed.
    "*Yaay!*"

Luna, bright as quicksilver, full of spooky fun, scoots under the sheets… zooms across the room! Dances on the ceiling!

Together, touched by magic, they
ride a moonlit breeze, to whoop and
tumble full of fun…above the shadowy trees.

Tumbling over and under they fly,
little ghost and child. Twirling,
whirling, two spinning raindrop
bubbles, shimmering and wild!

Little Luna and the child play ghost
games all through the night…joined
by creatures no longer afraid, till dawn
spreads a misty light.

Then back, back they fly. Back to the
house, to the cozy room…where the
little bed lies waiting.

The child cuddles and snuggles as
Luna flutters good-bye.
"Oooooo-ooooo . . ."

Shimmering, she floats back to her churchyard.

Tomorrow she will search again.
Softly, silently, she will drift…
searching for spooky fun.

Someone to play with in the mist….

Maybe you'll be the one!